The Rooftop Rocket Party

For Finn and Jon

Roland Chambers

A Neal Porter Book
ROARING BROOK PRESS
Brookfield, Connecticut

One summer Finn went to visit Doctor Gass in New York.

Doctor Gass was a famous rocket scientist.

But when Finn asked Doctor Gass where he *kept*
his rockets, the great man just smiled and said:

"In a very secret and unusual place."

There were no real rockets in Doctor Gass's laboratory, which was green and full of plans.

Or in his library, which was red and full of books.

There were no rockets at all in Central Park,
though Finn thought it would make
a terrific launchpad.

And although there were plenty in the Museum of Rocket
Science, none of them belonged to Doctor Gass . . .

DO NOT TOUCH

NASA

. . . which was a pity.

That evening, over dinner, Doctor Gass explained to Finn that the Moon moved around the Earth and was made of rock.

EARTH

P S

MOON

Plan no 67589

Moon

Earth

Sun

"I always thought the Moon was made of cheese," said Finn.
"The Moon is made of rock," said Doctor Gass.
"Then what does the Man in the Moon eat for his supper?"
wondered Finn.
"There is no supper on the Moon," said Doctor Gass,
"and what is more there is no Man in the Moon to eat it."
"Is that so?" asked Finn.
"That," replied Doctor Gass, "is a mathematical certainty."

"Oh," said Finn . . .

. . . and went to bed.

DO NOT
DISTURB

But at midnight, when everybody was asleep,
a Night Thing came tapping at his window.
"Good evening," said the Night Thing. "My master
is the Man in the Moon, and he has asked me to
invite you to his birthday party."

"But Doctor Gass says there is no Man in the Moon,"
said Finn.
"Is that so?" said the Night Thing.
"That," said Finn, "is a mathematical certainty."
The Night Thing just yawned and licked his chops.
"Twelve o'clock tomorrow night," he said. "Don't be late."

The next morning Finn told Doctor Gass
what had happened.

"But that was just a dream!"
said Doctor Gass.

And he explained how
dreams worked.

And went on explaining
until Finn begged him to stop.

That day they climbed the Empire State Building,
which was tall, but not *that* tall.

"How far away is the Moon?" asked Finn.
"The Moon," replied Doctor Gass,
"is 240,000 miles away."
"A long way," said Finn.
"An amazingly long way," said Doctor Gass.

"Gosh," said Finn . . .

. . . and they came
down again.

But on the way home he saw something that made him point
and shout, "Doctor Gass! I know where you hide your rockets!"

And there, on the rooftops, were big
red rockets, ready for liftoff!

"But those aren't rockets," laughed
Doctor Gass, "they're water tanks!"
And he explained how water towers held
water for people to drink, and to shower,
and to wash dishes now and then.

And he went on explaining
until Finn begged him
to stop.

That evening, Finn asked Doctor Gass where
he *did* keep his rockets.
"My rockets?" replied Doctor Gass, "Why, I keep
them in the most secret and unusual place of all . . .

. . . my *head*!!"

Finn was so disappointed that he went to bed
without touching his supper . . .

. . . which wasn't like Finn at all.

But at five minutes to twelve the Night Thing
came tapping at his window.

"Hurry!" he said.
"No time to dress . . ."

Up on the roof stood
his very own tower.

"Just remember," said the Night
Thing, "everyone in New York
has a rocket on his rooftop."

Liftoff!

Everybody was invited to the
Man in the Moon's birthday party.

When they landed,
the Man in the Moon
met them one by one.

"Good evening!" he said,
"and welcome."

"And now,
let the fun begin!"

First they played the bouncing game.

Finn bounced so high he thought he'd never come down again.

Next they hunted each other
through the moon caves,
which were all lit up with green.

When they were hungry
they had a picnic . . .

. . . which tasted like
nothing on Earth.

"But where is
the cheese?"
wondered Finn.

MOON SHINE

"I am sorry," replied
the Man in the Moon,
"I have eaten all the
cheese. Please have
a cream puff."

And then . . .

. . . when they were
all sleepy . . .

. . . and the night was
almost over . . .

. . . the Man in the Moon
played them a tune
on his pale violin.

Soon it was time
to go home.

The next morning Doctor Gass went
into his bathroom to brush his teeth.

But there was no water in the tap. Not a drop.

So he went outside in his
bathrobe to investigate.

And there he saw something so unmathematical . . .

. . so *very* unscientific . . .

. . . that he closed his eyes and said, "RIDICULOUS!"

It was a great red rocket parked
right in the middle of the street!

And close by, on the sidewalk,
was a half-eaten cream puff . . .

. . . which belonged to a little boy
who was fast asleep upstairs . . .

. . . because space travel
is very exhausting.

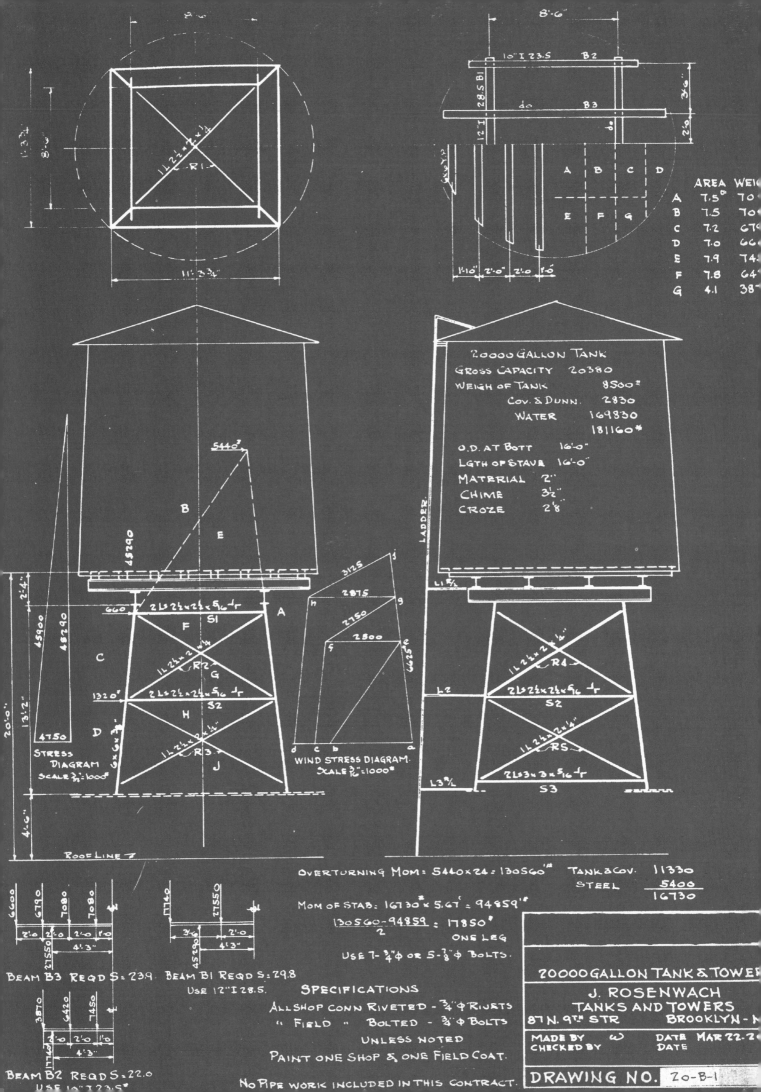